KW-484-272

THE
TROUBLE WITH
TRIANGLES

For Nat and Aggie—L.M.

To Adri and the adventures we shared growing up—B.M.

OXFORD
UNIVERSITY PRESS

Great Clarendon Street, Oxford OX2 6DP

Oxford University Press is a department of the University of Oxford.
It furthers the University's objective of excellence in research, scholarship,
and education by publishing worldwide. Oxford is a registered trade mark
of Oxford University Press in the UK and in certain other countries

Text copyright © Oxford University Press 2025
Illustrations copyright © Bia Melo 2025

The moral rights of the author have been asserted

Database right Oxford University Press (maker)

First published in 2025

All rights reserved. No part of this publication may be reproduced,
stored in a retrieval system, or transmitted, in any form or by any means,
without the prior permission in writing of Oxford University Press,
or as expressly permitted by law, or under terms agreed with the appropriate
reprographics rights organization. Enquiries concerning reproduction
outside the scope of the above should be sent to the Rights Department,
Oxford University Press, at the address above

You must not circulate this book in any other binding or cover
and you must impose this same condition on any acquirer

British Library Cataloguing in Publication Data

Data available

ISBN: 978-0-19-278770-5

1 3 5 7 9 10 8 6 4 2

Printed in China

The manufacturing process conforms to the
environmental regulations of the country of origin

FSC
www.fsc.org

MIX
Paper | Supporting
responsible forestry
FSC® C020056

Doodle and DOT

THE TROUBLE WITH TRIANGLES

Written by
Lily Murray

Illustrated by
Bia Melo

OXFORD
UNIVERSITY PRESS

Doodle and Dot are best friends. They do everything together. Most of all, they love making things. Today, they are drawing shapes.

What's your favourite shape, Dot? I love drawing rectangles.

My favourite shape is a square. All the best things are squares . . .

. . . chocolate, a magic box, presents . . .

Even though Doodle and Dot are best friends,
they don't ALWAYS agree.

Oh Dot, we forgot about
TRIANGLES! I LOVE triangles.
And with triangles we can create . . .
triangle aliens!

Doodle, no! Triangle
aliens sound like trouble!

But Doodle is now
having too much
fun drawing to
listen to Dot.

Just one more
triangle to add to
my rocket!

Doodle, stop!
I don't want to be
in a rocket!

3, 2, 1 . . . BLAST OFF!

Doodle and Dot are zooming through space . . . but can you see who else has come along for the ride?

Doodle is **very** excited to be in space.

The perfect place to draw stars! Space is brilliant!

Dot is **not happy** to be in space.

And someone is after his pencil!

Doodle and Dot need to watch out. The triangle alien is drawing lots of friends!

...a circle for the balloon ... Hooray! We're floating to safety! Squares and circles saved the day.

Soon Doodle and Dot have drawn a beautiful balloon! Dot adds some birds to the sky, but are those pointy triangle beaks a good idea?

Now the the dinosaur looks mean and fierce and HUNGRY!

I know what to draw!

The problem is, the dinosaur is eating the cookies faster than Doodle and Dot can draw them.

How are Doodle and Dot going to escape?

Quick, climb down this hole!

But triangles in the sea can only mean one thing . . . sharks!

Which shapes could Doodle and Dot use to get
away from the sharks?

Doodle and Dot are safe at last.

CAN YOU FIND ALL THESE SHAPES IN THE STORY?

stars

circles in space

cookie circle

triangle shark fins

rectangle
spaceship

square hot air
balloon basket

triangle spikes

circle hole